Spider Crusader

Spider Crusader

Destruction Of Zoomopolis

Josh Zimmer

Superstar Speedsters

The book has been inspired by other superhero franchises such as My Hero Academia, Marvel, DC, and Power Rangers!

CONTENTS

book

Spider Crusader was standing in Oasis Falls High School, and put his hand on Justin's healing tube. Spider Crusader said, "Don't worry, buddy, you will be healed soon, and will be back to full health." Police cars were zooming through the streets in the background with their sirens on. Spider Crusader said, "That's my queue to jump in to action!" Spider Crusader web swung out of the window, and web swung towards the police cars. Spider Crusader shot a web at the police cars and slingshot himself toward them. Spider Crusader landed on top of the police car, and kept his balance. The other car was speeding through the street, and bashed in to the police car. Spider Crusader said, "Hey bud, your driving skills are as bad as an pigeon on an bicycle." Spider Crusader shot an web at the other car's trunk, and pulled it open. Spider Crusader threw an web grenade at the trunk. The web grenade went in to the trunk, and exploded. The engine exploded in the other car, and caught on fire. The other car lost its control, and smashed in to the light post. The light post fell on top of the other car, and made the other car explode. The leader of the gang drove up next to the police car, and bashed the police car in to the wall. The police car smashed in to the building, and spun out of control. The building's foundation crumbled, and fell on top of the car. Spider Crusader's spider sense went off, and he jumped on to the gang leader's car. Spider Crusader landed on the hood of the gang leader's car. The gang leader got spooked, and started to drive recklessly. The car was speeding through the streets, and smashing in to everything. The citizens of Zoomopolis were running away, as the car was smashing through trash cans, buildings, and hot dog stands. Glass shards and trash were flying everywhere, as Spider Crusader was hanging on to the hood of the car. Spider Crusader punched the windshield with his fist, until it shattered. Glass shards from the windshield fell on to the road, as the car was driving crazily through the neighborhood. The gang leader grabbed his gun from the car seat, and started shooting it at Spider Crusader. Spider Crusader dodged the bullets, with his fast reflexes. Spider Crusader shot an web at the gun, and smashed it in to the car's window. The window shattered as the gun exploded. Spider Crusader shot an web at the gang leader's head, and pulled the gang leader toward him. Spider Crusader grabbed the gang leader's head, and bashed it against the steering wheel. Blood poured from the gang leader's head. Spider Crusader grabbed his web knife from his belt, and stabbed it in to the gang leader's neck. The gang leader laid dead on the steering wheel. The car horn went off, as the car drove in to the gas station, and exploded. Spider Crusader jumped off of the car's hood, and landed on the ground. The gas station was burning to the ground, as the fire trucks drove up to the scene. The fire trucks stopped at the fire, and the fire fighters washed the fire away with the water hose. Spider Crusader sat on the bench, and drank an bottle of water to rehydrate himself. Spider Crusader threw away the water bottle, and web swung through the city. Spider Crusader backflipped through the air, and landed at an middle school called Revolution Middle School. There was an group of kids in the middle of the courtyard. Spider Crusader walked toward the group of kids, and leaned next to the tree. Several students were in an circle around Daniel and Adam. Adam pushed Daniel on to the ground, and bent down over his body. Adam punched Daniel in the face, multiple times. Daniel's face was bleeding, as Adam growled and picked up Daniel's body. Adam threw Daniel in to the flag pole. Daniel smashed in to the flag pole, and rolled on the ground. Adam stepped on Daniel's chest, as Daniel coughed. Daniel coughed, while Adam was crushing him in to the ground. Spider Crusader shot an web at Adam's arm, and pulled him off of Daniel.

Adam stumbled backwards, as Spider Crusader back flipped and kicked Adam in the face. Spider Crusader punched Adam in the chest! Adam smashed against the tree. Spider Crusader web swung himself in to the tree, and kicked Adam in the chest. Adam smashed through the tree, and fell on to the ground. Spider Crusader picked up Adam's body, and smashed him on to the ground. The ground made an dent, as Adam laid on the ground. Daniel got up from the ground, and walked toward Spider Crusader. Daniel said, "Thanks for saving me!" Spider Crusader nodded and said, "No problem, I am here to protect the city and its citizens." Adam got up, and rubbed his head. Adam sat on the school steps, and lowered his head. Spider Crusader and Daniel walked down the street toward Daniel's house. Daniel's house was an blue house with a nice garden. Daniel and Spider Crusader walked toward the front door, and rang the door bell. Daniel's dad, Zach, let Daniel and Spider Crusader in to the house. Daniel and Spider Crusader sat on the couch together. The doorbell rang, and Zach opened the door. Norman was at the front door, on his glider. Norman hovered in to the house on his glider. Zach closed the door and said, "What a beautiful day outside!" Norman said, "It is an beautiful day!" Spider Crusader's spider sense went off, and he got up from the couch with Daniel. Daniel and Spider Crusader walked down the hallway. Spider Crusader and Daniel stopped at the bathroom! Daniel opened the bathroom door, and walked in to it. Spider Crusader locked the door for the bathroom. Daniel said, "Why did you lock the bathroom door?" Spider Crusader said, "It is for your safety!" Spider Crusader walked down the hallway, and spied on Zach and Norman. Norman said, "I am an simple man, that likes to do business!" Zach said, "What does this have to do with me?" Norman said, "There is an colorful pest swinging around the city! He is known as Spider Crusader, and he has been destroying my creations for an while." Zach said, "I am not going to endanger my family, by helping you hunt down superheroes." Norman growled and said, "I don't care about your family, my business is being destroyed by this pest." Zach said, "If you don't care about my family, then get out of my house." Zach swung his arm at Norman. Norman grabbed Zach's arm, and kicked him in the chest. Zach slid backwards! Norman laughed and said, "Attempting to punch me is your first mistake!" Norman grabbed Zach's arm! Norman twisted Zach's arm, and pulled it behind Zach's back. Zach screamed in pain! Norman laughed, as he smashed Zach in to the ground. Zach laid on the ground! Norman took a container off of his belt, and a needle. Norman loaded the liquid from the container in to the needle. Norman stabbed the needle in to Zach's arm. Zach struggled on the ground, as the liquid turned his body in to an monster made out of molten lava. Spider Crusader's spider sense went off! Norman said, "I can sense the spider in the area! Molten Monster, deal with the pest, while I capture the kid." Norman walked on to his glider, and hovered past Spider Crusader to find Daniel. Norman hovered down the hallway, and stopped at the bathroom. Norman grabbed an pumpkin bomb from his belt, and attached it to the door. The pumpkin bomb exploded, and the door opened. Daniel was terrified in fear, and sitting in the corner. Norman electrocuted Daniel with his electric taser! Daniel was electrocuted with electric energy. Daniel passed out on the ground. Norman picked up Daniel's body, and laid him on his shoulder. Norman walked on to the glider, and hovered out of the bathroom. Norman flew down the hallway on his glider. Norman flew in to the living room. Norman said, "I have captured the kid, meet me back at the secret hideout, after you deal with the spider." Molten Monster said, "Yes Master!" Norman flew out of the front door, and toward his secret hideout. Spider Crusader shot a web at Molten Monster. Molten Monster grabbed the web, and pulled Spider Crusader toward him. Molten Monster punched Spider Crusader in the chest. Spider Crusader smashed in to the wall, and laid next to it. Molten Monster charged toward the wall, and tackled Spider Crusader. Molten Monster body slammed Spider Crusader in to the ground, and punched him in the face. Spider Crusader's armor absorbed most of the heat from Molten Monster's arms. Molten Monster growled, as he tried to punch through Spider Crusader's armor. Spider Crusader said, "You need an breath mint, your breath is too hot!" Spider Crusader shot an web at Molten Monster's face. Molten Monster growled in anger, as he melted the web off of his face. Spider Crusader back flipped off of the ground. Spider Crusader shot his web at an book shelf, and threw it at Molten Monster. Molten Monster punched the book shelf, and smashed it to pieces. Molten Monster sped toward Spider Crusader, and grabbed him. Molten Monster wrapped his arms around Spider Crusader, and heated up his body. Spider Crusader said, "Awwwww, you must be an softie, since you like to give out bear hugs." Molten Monster's body ignited an explosion of molten energy. The explosion covered the area, and the house exploded. The house's foundation collapsed on top of Spider Crusader, as he laid on the ground. Spider Crusader got up from the ground, and rubbed his head. The foundation pieces of the house, fell on to the ground, as Spider Crusader got up. Molten Monster smiled, and kicked Spider Crusader in the chest. Spider Crusader slid backwards, and laid next to the car, that was in the middle of the road. Police cars stopped in front of the Molten Monster. Police officers climbed out of the police cars, and started shooting at the Molten Monster. Spider Crusader said, "No, stay back! He is too dangerous for you to handle!" Molten Monster growled, and ignited an explosion from his body. The explosion made the police cars explode, and the police officers laid on the ground in puddles of blood. Spider Crusader laid on the ground, catching his breath. Spider Crusader said, "Police officers are idiots, they never listen to superheroes." Molten Monster walked closer to Spider Crusader, and kicked him in the chest. Spider Crusader rolled on the ground. Molten Monster grabbed Spider Crusader's leg, and threw him in to the pole. The pole fell on to the ground, as Spider Crusader rolled on the ground. Molten Monster walked closer to Spider Crusader. Spider Crusader laid on the ground, and thought of the best strategy to defeat Molten Monster. Spider Crusader shot an web at the ice cream stand. The web attached to the ice cream, and froze the webs in the web shooters in to an shard of ice. Spider Crusader grabbed the fire hydrant next to him, and pulled it out of the ground. The water from the fire hydrant splashed on to the road, and continued splashing water out in to the air. Spider Crusader shot a web at Molten Monster, and a web at the water. The webs froze the water and Molten Monster in to an huge pillar of ice. Spider Crusader got up from the ground, and picked up an car. Spider Crusader threw the car at the frozen Molten Monster. The Molten Monster exploded in to shards of ice. Spider Crusader sat on the bench to catch his breath. Down the street, Norman flew in to his secret hideout, with Daniel on his glider. Norman landed his glider in the secret hideout, and opened up his experiment machine. Norman laid Daniel in to his experiment machine, and attached the wires to Daniel's body. Norman closed the machine! Norman logged on to his computer, and turned on the machine. The machine spun its gears, and sent electric energy in to Daniel's body. The electric energy tortured Daniel by electrocuting his body. Norman laughed manically, at the computer, as the machine tortured Daniel. An woman walked in to the secret hideout with an black latex suit. The woman was Fiona, and she was an high ranked burglar, that can outsmart anyone in her league. Fiona walked toward Norman, and leaned on his chair. Fiona said, "Working on your usual experiments, Norman?" Norman said, "Yep, I am having fun, by torturing him." Fiona said, "Good, I like it when my victims scream in pain and terror." Fiona rubbed some chap stick on her lips, as she played with Norman's hair. Fiona said, "I heard that we have an problem with an colorful spider." Norman said, "Yep, he has defeated our recent henchman, Molten Monster." Fiona said, "I am going to play with the little spider." Norman said, "Be careful, he is an slippery little pest." Fiona back flipped out of the window for the secret hideout, and landed on the ground. Fiona jumped on to the speeding police car, and rode it to the bank. The speeding police car sped down the street, and zoomed past Spider Crusader. Spider Crusader got up from the bench, and shot an web at the police car. Fiona crawled from the trunk of the police car, and jumped through the window. Fiona landed in the car, and stabbed the police officer in the neck with her knife. The police officer laid on the floor of the police car, while Fiona took over the steering wheel. Spider Crusader pulled on the web, and launched himself on to the hood of the police car. The police car sped through the streets, and crashed through various items. Fiona steered the police car, and tried to shake Spider Crusader off of the hood of the police car. Spider Crusader hung on to the hood of the police car. Fiona recklessly drove the police car. The police car was running over trash cans, and food stands, while running over panicking citizens. The bodies of the citizens laid on the road in puddles of blood. The piles of trash, and flying food was bouncing off of Spider Crusader, as he hung on to the police car. Spider Crusader crawled on to the windshield, and smashed his fist through it. The windshield shattered, as Fiona panicked. Fiona steered the police car in to an light pole. The light pole fell on to the road, as Spider Crusader crawled in to the car. Spider Crusader roundhouse kicked Fiona in the face. Fiona tumbled out of the car, and rolled in to the road. Spider Crusader jumped out of the car. Fiona grabbed her taser off of her belt, and electrocuted Spider Crusader. Spider Crusader fell backwards, as Fiona got up from the ground. Fiona kicked Spider Crusader in the chest. Spider Crusader slid backwards in to the wall. Fiona walked to Spider Crusader, and rubbed her hand on his body. Fiona said, "Hello, hot shot, would you retract your helmet for an wonderful woman like me?" Spider Crusader nervously laid next to the wall. Fiona rubbed her hand on Spider Crusader's chest. Fiona said, "Don't be nervous, you're the hottest superhero in Zoomopolis." Spider Crusader retracted his helmet. Fiona said, "You're an good boy!" Fiona kissed Spider Crusader on the cheek. Spider Crusader blushed, as Fiona rubbed his arm. Fiona licked her lips and said, "You are so strong and brave. I like superheroes, who are strong and brave." Fiona kissed Spider Crusader on the lips. Fiona said, "I have an favor to ask?" Spider Crusader said, "What is the favor?" Fiona said, "There is an community gym, with a swimming pool down the street." Spider Crusader said, "Your favor is that you want to go swimming with me?" Fiona smiled and said, "Yes, you are an smart boy!" Fiona ruffled up Spider Crusader's hair, and kissed him on the cheek. Fiona hung on to Spider Crusader's back, as he web swung down the street. Spider Crusader and Fiona landed at the community gym, and walked in to it. Spider Crusader and Fiona walked toward the swimming pool. Spider Crusader and Fiona stood in front of the swimming pool. Fiona pressed an button on her wrist, and her uniform transformed in to an bathing suit. Spider Crusader pressed an button on his belt, and his suit retracted. The suit transformed in to an bathing suit. Fiona saw Spider Crusader's body, and was amazed. Fiona said, "You are so hot, Peter!" Peter blushed, as he nervously smiled. Peter said, "Thanks!" Fiona said, "Don't be nervous, we are here to have fun." Peter and Fiona ran toward the swimming pool, and jumped in to it. Peter and Fiona splashed each other in the swimming pool. Fiona and Peter swam laps around the swimming pool. Peter and Fiona got out of the swimming pool, and sat on the edge of the swimming pool together. Fiona and Peter hugged and kissed each other. Fiona said, "You are fun to hang out with, little spider!" Peter smiled and said, "You are fun to hang out with as well." Fiona ruffled Peter's hair. Fiona's wrist communicator started to go off. Fiona said, "I need to take this call." Peter brushed his hair and said, "Don't worry, I will sit here, and wait for you." Fiona got up, and tapped the button on her wrist communicator. Fiona laid next to the wall. Norman said, "Are you having fun playing with the little spider?" Fiona said, "Yes, what's up?" Norman said, "I need more blood from Spider Crusader for my experiments, can you get me some more?" Fiona said, "That shouldn't be an problem, I have him tangled up in my web" Norman said, "Good, don't fail me!" Fiona said, "I won't!" Fiona pressed an button on her wrist communicator, and ended the conversation. Peter was sitting on the edge of the pool. Fiona walked over to Peter, and sat next to him. Fiona said, "Do you mind, if I take some of your blood? My boss needs it for his experiments." Peter said, "I don't mind at all, I would do anything for you." Fiona smiled, as she took a needle and an canister out of her pocket. Fiona attached the canister to the needle. Peter laid his arm in Fiona's lap. Fiona stabbed the needle in to Peter's arm. Peter's blood poured in to the canister. The canister filled to the top, and Fiona took the needle out of Peter's arm. Fiona sealed the canister with a lid, and put it in her pocket. Fiona took an towel out of her pocket, and wiped the left over blood from Peter's arm. Fiona put an band aid on Peter's arm to stop the bleeding. Fiona said, "Thanks hot shot, you're the best." Fiona kissed Peter's cheek, as Peter blushed. Fiona and Peter got up from the edge of the swimming pool. Fiona pressed an button on her wrist, and her suit covered up her body. Peter pressed an button on his wrist, and his armor covered his body. Peter gave Fiona an spider drone. Peter said, "This will keep track of your location." Fiona grabbed the spider drone, and attached it to her belt. The spider drone activated, and the GPS signal showed up on Peter's wrist communicator. Fiona smiled and walked out of the gym. Fiona said, "Keep being awesome, hot shot." Peter smiled back at Fiona. Fiona stood outside the gym, and pressed an button on her wrist. Fiona's glider flew toward her, and landed in front of the gym. Fiona walked on to her glider, and flew toward Norman's secret hideout. Peter walked out of the gym, and web swung around the city. Spider Crusader followed Fiona's GPS signal, and landed outside the secret hideout. Spider Crusader slowly walked toward the security gate, and hid next to the wall. Fiona landed in front of the secret hideout, and pressed an button on her wrist. Fiona's glider flew in to the secret hideout, and landed in the recharge station. Fiona walked through the security gate, and scanned her security card on the panel. Spider Crusader web crawled on the wall, and followed Fiona. Fiona walked through the hallway of the secret hideout. Spider Crusader web crawled on the ceiling, and avoided the security cameras. Spider Crusader webbed the security cameras with his web shooters, and destroyed them. Fiona walked in to Norman's office! Spider Crusader web crawled in to Norman's office. Spider Crusader jumped off of the wall, and hid behind the book shelf in Norman's office. Fiona walked toward Norman. Norman was at his computer, logging data in to the computer's database. Fiona took the canister of Spider Crusader's blood off of her belt, and laid it next to Norman. Norman smiled, and picked up the canister of Spider Crusader's blood. Norman attached the canister of Spider Crusader's blood to his DNA machine, and pressed the button on the machine. The machine scanned the canister of Spider Crusader's blood, and uploaded the DNA to Norman's computer. Norman saved the DNA results in to the computer's database. Norman noticed that the environment felt off. Norman waved his hand in the air. Norman's security guards saw the signal, and patrolled the area. Fiona walked out of Norman's office, and laid next to the wall. Spider Crusader laid his hand on the wall, and quietly walked around the area. Norman's security guards saw Spider Crusader, and walked behind him. Spider Crusader's spider sense went off, as Norman's security guards stopped behind Spider Crusader. Norman's security guards tackled Spider Crusader, and held him on the ground. Spider Crusader growled, as the security guards electrocuted Spider Crusader with their tasers. Spider Crusader screamed in pain, as he laid on the ground. One of Norman's security guards picked up Spider Crusader, and wrapped their arms around him. Spider Crusader struggled in the security guard's grip, as they walked toward Norman. One of Norman's security guards said, "We found an intruder in your office." Norman smiled and said, "It's the little spider, that likes to ruin my operations." Spider Crusader said, "Your ego is as big as an inflated balloon." Norman growled, and walked over to Spider Crusader. Norman punched Spider Crusader in the face! Norman said, "You better watch your tongue, little spider. You don't want to piss me off." Spider Crusader said, "Awwwwww, the villain's ego is going to explode" Norman growled, and grabbed Spider Crusader by his neck. Norman lifted Spider Crusader in to the air, and smashed him through the table. Spider Crusader laid on the ground. Norman stepped on Spider crusader's chest, and held him on the ground. Norman said, "This is your last chance, spider, watch your mouth, or you will regret messing with me!" Spider Crusader said, "I can handle anything that you throw at me!" Spider Crusader shot an web in Norman's face. The web attached to Norman's face! Spider Crusader slid backwards, and backflipped off of the ground. Norman growled, as he ripped the web off of his face. Spider Crusader shot a web at Norman's chest. Spider Crusader slingshot himself in to Norman, and kicked him in to the wall. Norman smashed in to the wall, and stumbled backwards. Spider Crusader back flipped, and kicked Norman in the face. Norman growled, and grabbed Spider Crusader's leg. Norman smashed Spider Crusader in to the ground multiple times, and threw him in to the table, that was filled with multiple containers. Spider Crusader smashed through multiple glass containers, and rolled on the ground. Glass shards from the containers fell on to the ground. Spider Crusader backflipped off of the ground, and shot some webs at Norman. The webs bounced off of Norman's chest, as Norman walked toward Spider Crusader. Spider Crusader was terrified in fear, as he slowly walked backwards. Norman walked closer to Spider Crusader! Norman said, "What's wrong, little spider, are you scared that your webs don't work on me?" Spider Crusader said, "I am not scared of you!" Norman grabbed a explosive bomb from his belt, and threw it at Spider Crusader. Spider Crusader shot a web at the bomb, and threw it back at Norman. The bomb exploded, and Norman barely moved an inch. Norman said, "Silly spider, my own weapons don't hurt me!" Norman grabbed Spider Crusader by his neck, and smashed him in to the wall. Spider Crusader's body left an dent on the wall, as Spider Crusader was trying to get out of Norman's grip. Norman smashed Spider Crusader in to the wall multiple times. The wall cracked, as Spider Crusader growled. Norman lifted Spider Crusader in to the air, and smashed him in to the ground. Spider Crusader laid on the ground, as Norman smiled. Norman held Spider Crusader on the ground, as Spider Crusader tried to catch his breath. Norman said, "The spider is battered and bruised, you should surrender, while you have the chance." Spider Crusader growled and said, "Heroes never give up, when their enemy has the upper hand." Norman said, "Those are lame words for an worthless spirit." Spider Crusader lifted his arm, and tried to shoot a web at Norman's face. Norman grabbed Spider Crusader's arm, and lifted him in the air. Norman said, "Your little webs can't save you this time, spider!" Norman punched Spider Crusader in the face. Spider Crusader smashed in to the wall, and laid on the ground, as his helmet shattered to pieces. Spider Crusader got up from the ground, and crawled on the walls! Spider Crusader's spider senses were going crazy, since the stakes have gotten pretty high for the situation. Norman said, "The spider is running away like a little scared cat, how pathetic." Spider Crusader grabbed a web bomb from his belt, and threw it at Norman. The web bomb exploded, and Norman slid backwards! Spider Crusader crawled on the wall, and shot a web at the door panel. The door panel exploded, as the door opened. Spider Crusader crawled to the door, and back flipped through it. Norman pressed the emergency button on the wall, and put the hideout in Red Alert. Security robots rolled in to the hallway, and surrounded Spider Crusader, as the door to Norman's office automatically closed behind him. The security robots were shooting at Spider Crusader. Spider Crusader grabbed web bombs from his belt, and threw them at the security robots. The web bombs exploded, and robot parts flew everywhere. Spider Crusader ran through the hallway, as more security robots chased after him. The security robots shot rockets at Spider Crusader. The rockets hit Spider Crusader in the back, and Spider Crusader smashed in to the wall. The security robots rolled toward Spider Crusader, as he got up from the ground. The security robots shot wires at Spider Crusader. The wires wrapped around Spider Crusader's body, and electrocuted him. Spider Crusader growled in pain, as he laid on the ground. The security robots punched Spider Crusader in the chest, as he laid on the ground. One of the security robots picked up Spider Crusader by his neck, and lifted him in to the air. Spider Crusader growled, as the security robot punched Spider Crusader in the chest multiple times. Spider Crusader growled, as his armor absorbed the damage. The security robot smashed Spider Crusader in to the wall, multiple times. Spider Crusader growled, and attached a web bomb from his belt to the security robot's chest. The web bomb exploded, and the security robot lost their grip on Spider Crusader. Spider Crusader landed on the ground, as the security robot exploded. The security camera was pointing at Spider Crusader. Spider Crusader disabled the camera with his webs, and ran through the hallway. Spider Crusader made it in to the next section of the hallway, as he stopped to catch his breath. The security guard walked toward Spider Crusader. Spider Crusader shot his webs at the security guard. The security guard swung his electric sword at the webs, and sliced them in half. The security guard sped toward Spider Crusader, and kicked him in the chest. Spider Crusader slid backwards. Spider Crusader grabbed the security guard's arm, and shot an web in the security guard's face. The security guard growled and swung his electric sword. Spider Crusader tried to dodge the electric sword. The security guard stabbed Spider Crusader in the chest, with the electric sword. Spider Crusader got electrocuted, as he growled in pain. The security guard kicked Spider Crusader in the chest. Spider Crusader rolled on the ground. Spider Crusader grabbed an web bomb from his belt, and threw it at the security guard. The web bomb exploded, and the security guard smashed in to the wall. The security guard dropped his electric sword. Spider Crusader back flipped off of the ground. Spider Crusader tacked the security guard, and held them on the wall. Spider Crusader stabbed his web knife in to the security guard's neck. The security guard laid on the ground in an puddle of blood. Spider Crusader web swung further in to the hallway. Spider Crusader saw the entrance to the villain hideout, and was relived that he was almost out of the madness. Security turrets guarded the entrance. Spider Crusader's spider senses went off, as the turrets shot at him. Spider Crusader flipped in to the air, and shot webs at the turrets. Spider Crusader ran through the entrance, and made it outside, as the doors closed behind him. Spider Crusader was catching his breath, as Fiona walked toward him. Fiona said, "Hey hot shot, looks like you just made it out of an tough maze!" Spider Crusader was relived to see Fiona, as he walked over to her. Spider Crusader said, "It was crazy in there. There was an psychopath named Norman, and he tried to kill me." Fiona hugged Spider Crusader and said, "Oh my, that is awful!" Spider Crusader hugged Fiona back and said, "I know, it is awful." Fiona said, "To make you feel better, let me take you to my place for some relaxation." Spider Crusader said, "Sounds great, I need some relaxation!" Fiona climbed on to Spider Crusader's back, and hung on to him. Spider Crusader web swung in to the air. Spider Crusader web swung to Fiona's house. Spider Crusader landed on the ground. Fiona got off of Spider Crusader's back, and stepped on to the ground. Fiona and Spider Crusader walked in to Fiona's house. Fiona's house was huge, and it was filled with technology, and various gadgets. Fiona and Spider Crusader sat on the couch together. Fiona wrapped her arm around Spider Crusader's back, as they relaxed together. Spider Crusader retracted his helmet. The helmet uncovered Spider Crusader's face! Fiona and Spider Crusader kissed each other on the couch. Spider Crusader pressed the button on his helmet. The helmet covered Spider Crusader's face. Spider Crusader got up from the couch. Fiona said, "Is everything ok?" Spider Crusader said, "I sense an threat is on the horizon at Oasis Falls High School. Fiona said, "Be safe!" Spider Crusader said, "I will try to be safe!" Spider Crusader shot an web at the window, and pulled it open. Spider Crusader climbed out of the window, and jumped out of it. Spider Crusader landed on the ground. Spider Crusader shot an web at the window, and pulled on the web to close it. Spider Crusader web swung in to the air to Oasis Falls High School. Down the street at the villain hideout, Norman was cleaning the debris from his laboratory. Norman said, "I wish the pest would just go away! He likes to ruin all of my gadgets and fun." Daniel was in the experiment tube, and overheard Norman talking to himself. Daniel said, "Spider Crusader keeps breaking your toys, because you like to mess up Zoomopolis." Norman said, "Shut up, no one asked you, you're my captive!" Norman electrocuted Daniel with his remote. Daniel screamed in pain, as the wires electrocuted him. Norman said, "You are my new toy, and you will obey me!" Norman pressed an button on his computer, and Spider Crusader's blood poured in to the wires from the container, that was attached to the computer. Spider Crusader's blood was injected in to Daniel through the wires. Norman injected some ghost powers in to the wires. The ghost powers flowed in to Daniel's body through the wires. Daniel's eyes glowed green, as he laid in the machine. Daniel's body ignited an explosion! The explosion made the experiment machine explode, and Daniel walked through the debris, as his eyes glowed green. Norman said, "I control you, follow my commands!" Norman pressed the button on his remote, as the signal does nothing to Daniel. Daniel walked toward Norman, with his eyes glowing green. Daniel shoots an energy beam from his hand! The energy beam destroys the remote in Norman's hand. Daniel said, "No one controls me, I am my own being." Norman threw an glass container at Daniel. Daniel went invisible, as he walked closer to Norman. The glass container went through Daniel, and smashed against the wall. Daniel's body went back to normal. Daniel said, "Nothing can hurt me, I am part ghost." Daniel went in to his ghost form, and flew in to Norman. Daniel smashed Norman in to the wall. Daniel's eyes glowed green, as he did an ghostly wail from his mouth. Norman smashed through the wall. Daniel towered over him. Daniel said, "None of your gadgets work on me!" Norman said, "I am your master, you can't beat me with your powers." Norman grabbed an electric baton from his belt, and electrocuted Daniel. Daniel's ghost powers malfunctioned, as he screamed in pain. Norman kicked Daniel in the chest. Daniel slid backwards! Norman got up from the ground, and punched Daniel in the face. Daniel smashed in to the table, and laid on the ground. Norman walked closer to Daniel. Daniel slowly got up from the ground. Norman said, "Don't bother fighting back, I have plenty of electric bombs to keep you down." Norman threw an electric bomb at Daniel. The electric bomb hit Daniel in the chest! The electric bomb exploded, and hit Daniel with electric energy. The electric energy electrocuted Daniel, as he screamed in pain. Daniel laid on the ground, as he tried to catch his breath. Norman walked closer to Daniel. Daniel got up from the ground, and shot an energy blast from his arms at Norman. Norman got hit by the energy blast, and smashed in to the wall. Daniel went in to his ghost form, and flew toward Norman. Daniel went invisible, and smashed Norman through multiple walls. Daniel phased through the walls, and smashed Norman out of the villain hideout. Norman laid on the ground, as Daniel's body went back to normal. Daniel stood over Norman, as his eyes glowed green. Daniel said, "Surrender, Norman, I am stronger than you." Norman said, "I can't be beaten by my own pawn." Daniel growled, as he grabbed Norman by his throat. Daniel lifted Norman in to the air and said, "I am not your pawn!" Daniel threw Norman in to the air. Daniel back flipped, and kicked Norman in the chest. Norman smashed in to the wall. Daniel shot an energy blast from his arm at Norman. The energy blast smashed Norman through the wall. Norman laid on the ground, as the building crumbled on top of him. Daniel said, "Be an good little dog, and stay down. If you don't stay down, I will kill you." Daniel went in to his ghost form, and flew toward Oasis Falls High School. Norman slowly got up from the ground, and caught his breath. He wiped the building debris off of his body. Norman said, "Daniel thinks that, I am down for the count, but what he doesn't know that I have multiple tricks up my sleeve." Norman was disappointed that his hideout was destroyed. Norman said, "All of my wonderful experiments are gone, but villains can easily climb back up from the bottom." Norman pressed an button on his wrist, and his glider flew toward him. Norman's glider landed in front of him. Norman walked on to his glider, and flew in to the air. Norman checked the tracker on his glider. Norman said, "Daniel is heading toward Oasis Falls High School. I will follow him, since the spider will probably be in the area as well." Norman flew toward Oasis Falls High School. Daniel used his ghost powers to control the street lights in Zoomopolis, while he flew toward Oasis Falls High School. The street lights went crazy, as the ghost powers controlled them. The street lights were flashing, as the cars sped through the streets, and crashed in to various buildings and the other objects in the city. Daniel laughed, as the chaos brewed through Zoomopolis. Daniel saw Oasis Falls High School in the distance, as he flew toward the courtyard. Daniel landed in the courtyard, and walked toward the doors of Oasis Falls High School. The security guard was standing in front of the doors. Daniel walked toward the security guard, and lifted him in to the air with his ghost powers from his hands. Daniel threw the security guard in to the flag pole. Daniel used his ghost wail on the security guard. The flag pole and the security guard flew across the street, and smashed through the building. The building crumbled on top of the security guard. Daniel smiled, as he blasted the doors open with his ghost powers. Daniel walked through the doors, and walked through the hallways. Oasis Falls High School looked empty, but Daniel's ghost sense has detected that there were students in the building. Daniel walked toward the teacher's lounge. Daniel saw the door for the teacher's lounge, and looked through the little window on the door. Daniel saw the teachers hiding in the room. Daniel kicked open the door, and broke the lock on the door. Daniel walked in to the teacher's lounge, and scanned the area for the teachers with his ghost vision. The teachers were hiding under the table. Daniel picked up the table and threw it at the wall. The table smashed to pieces, when it hit the wall. Daniel did an ghost wail! The teacher's lounge shook from the ghost wail, and the teachers smashed in to the wall. The teachers laid on the ground in puddles of blood. Daniel smiled, as he walked out of the teacher's lounge. Daniel walked down the hallway, and noticed that the students were terrified in fear, as they hid in the bathroom. Daniel shot an blast of ghost energy from his hand at the students in the bathroom. The students laid on the bathroom floor in puddles of blood. Daniel said, "It is fun to cause chaos!" Daniel walked toward the gym, and noticed that the gym was full of students. Daniel walked in to the gym, and leaned against the wall, as he saw the football team sitting on the stands, watching the cheerleaders practice their routine. The cheerleaders flipped in the air, and landed on the gym floor, as the football team cheered and clapped their hands. The cheerleaders bowed, and walked in to the coach's office to change in to their student clothes. Outside the school, Spider Crusader web swung on to the rooftop of Oasis Falls High School. Spider Crusader landed on the rooftop, and walked toward the vents. Spider Crusader pulled open the vents, and crawled in to them. Spider Crusader crawled in to the vents, and crawled to the vent, that was attached to the gym. Spider Crusader pulled open the vent, and crawled out of it. Spider Crusader hung backwards, and lowered himself in to the gym with one of his webs. Daniel saw Spider Crusader, and shot a ghost blast at the web. The web snapped, and Spider Crusader landed on to the gym floor. Daniel said, "You little pest, are you trying to ruin my fun?" Daniel shot ghost blasts at Spider Crusader. Spider Crusader back flipped over the blasts and said, "That's part of my job description." Spider Crusader shot webs at Daniel! Daniel made his body invisible, as the webs went through him. Daniel smirked and said, "You missed, hot shot!" Daniel did an ghost wail at Spider Crusader! Spider Crusader slid backwards in to the wall. Daniel went in to his ghost form, and flew in to Spider Crusader. Spider Crusader smashed in to the wall. Spider Crusader swung his arm at Daniel. Daniel's body went invisible. Daniel grabbed Spider Crusader's neck, and flew in to the air. Daniel threw Spider Crusader in to the ground, and blasted him in the chest with an ghost blast. Spider Crusader smashed in to the ground, and made an dent in the gym. Daniel flew toward Spider Crusader. Spider Crusader pulled himself backwards with an web! Daniel landed on the ground! Spider Crusader shot electric webs at Daniel. The electric webs electrocuted Daniel, as he slid backwards. Daniel said, "That tickled, do you have any more toys to annoy me with?" Spider Crusader said, "I have plenty of toys to show you!" Daniel said, "Prove it, hero!" Daniel waved his hands, and his ghost powers possessed the football team, that were in the gym. Daniel snapped his fingers, and the football team walked toward Daniel. Daniel used his ghost powers to control the football team. The football team growled, and charged at Spider Crusader. The football team tackled Spider Crusader in to the ground, and held him on the gym's floor. The football team punched Spider Crusader in the chest. Spider Crusader ignited an web explosion from his body. The football team got webbed on to the wall, as the ghost powers disconnected from their bodies. Spider Crusader growled, as he got up from the ground. Spider Crusader said, "You need an better strategy, ghost boy!" Daniel growled, as he flew towards Spider Crusader. Spider Crusader back flipped, and shot an web at Daniel's back. Spider Crusader pulled on the web, and threw Daniel in to the wall. Daniel smashed in to the wall, and laid next to it. Spider Crusader ran toward Daniel. Daniel used his ghost wail on Spider Crusader. Spider Crusader smashed in to the wall. Daniel flew toward Spider Crusader, and grabbed him by the neck. Daniel flew in to the air, and smashed Spider Crusader in to the basketball net. Spider Crusader laid in the basketball net. Daniel shot an ghost blast at the basketball net. The basketball net smashed in to the ground, and laid on top of Spider Crusader. Spider Crusader got up from the ground, as Daniel landed. The walls of Oasis Falls High School shook, as an missile smashed through the windows, and hit the gym walls. The missile exploded, as debris flew everywhere. Daniel and Spider Crusader laid on the ground, as debris fell on top of them. Norman laughed, as his glider landed in the middle of the debris. Norman said, "Two little bugs laying on the ground, in front of my feet." Norman walked off of his glider, and looked at the debris. Norman said, "The ghost boy and the spider in the same room, laying on the ground defeated. It must be my lucky day!" Daniel and Spider Crusader got up from the ground, and rubbed their heads. Norman said, "You guys must have had an good nap, because it is time for round 2 of pain." Norman laughed, as Daniel and Spider Crusader walked backwards. Norman said, "Showing fear makes you weak and worthless." Norman walked closer to Spider Crusader and Daniel, as he pressed an button on his wrists. The gloves on his hands started to glow, as they activated anti gravity mode. Norman lifted his hands in the air, and the anti gravity activated in the room. Daniel and Spider Crusader lifted in to the air. Norman waved his arms around, and smashed Daniel and Spider Crusader in to his other. Norman pressed an button on his gloves, and the anti gravity pulled Daniel and Spider Crusader toward him. Norman punched Spider Crusader and Daniel in the chest with an anti gravity explosion from his gloves. Spider Crusader and Daniel smashed in to the wall, and laid next to the wall, as they regained their balance. Norman laughed and said, "The bugs are trembling in fear, how pathetic."

Norman pressed an button on his wrist, and he teleported behind Spider Crusader and Daniel. Norman grabbed Daniel and Spider Crusader by their neck, and smashed both of them in to the ground. Norman stood on top of Daniel and Spider Crusader, as he crushed them in to the ground. Daniel and Spider Crusader growled, as Norman held them on the ground. Norman said, "Zoomopolis must be so pathetic, if they believed in you to protect them." Daniel and Spider Crusader ignited explosions of energy from their body. The room shook from the explosion, as Norman fell on the ground, and laid next to the wall. Daniel and Spider Crusader got up from the ground. Norman threw an electric bomb at Daniel and Spider Crusader. Spider Crusader and Daniel got electrocuted, as they slid back to the wall. Norman pressed an button on his wrist and summoned his glider. Norman jumped on to his glider, and flew through Oasis Falls High School, toward the recovery room. The recovery room is where Justin is stored in his healing tube. Daniel went in to his ghost form, and flew after Norman. Spider Crusader web swung, and followed Daniel. Norman flew in to the recovery room, and looked for Justin's healing tube. Norman found Justin's healing tube, and flew closer to it. Daniel flew in to the recovery room. Spider Crusader web swung in to the recovery room. Spider Crusader said, "Keep the healing tube away from Norman." Daniel nodded and flew toward the healing tube. Norman grabbed electric bombs from his belt, and threw them at Daniel. Daniel dodged the electric bombs, by flying around them. Daniel grabbed the healing tube, and turned invisible. Daniel flew in to the basement of Oasis Falls High School, and hid the healing tube in the basement closet. Daniel flew out of the basement, and flew back in to the recovery room. Norman got angry, and threw an electric bomb at Spider Crusader. Daniel landed in front of the electric bomb, and pushed it back at Norman with his ghost wail. Norman got electrocuted, and slid backwards. Spider Crusader shot an web at Norman, and launched himself in to Norman with the web. Spider Crusader punched Norman in the face. Norman slid backwards. Daniel flew towards Norman, and swung his arm at Norman.

Norman grabbed Daniel's arm, and lifted him in to the air. Norman punched Daniel in the face. Daniel flew through the air, and smashed in to Spider Crusader. Spider Crusader and Daniel toppled on to the ground. Norman lifted an shelf, and smashed it on top of Daniel and Spider Crusader, multiple times. The shelf shattered, as Daniel and Spider Crusader laid on the ground. Norman pressed an button on his wrist, and all of the electronics exploded in the recovery room, and electrocuted Daniel and Spider Crusader with the electric energy. Daniel and Spider Crusader screamed in pain, as Norman maniacally laughed. Norman pressed an button on his wrist, and summoned his glider. Norman jumped on to his glider, as it flew toward him. Norman grabbed an couple of electric bombs from his belt, and rolled them toward Spider Crusader and Daniel. The bombs exploded in front of Spider Crusader and Daniel. The explosion smashed Spider Crusader and Daniel in to the wall, as they got electrocuted. Spider Crusader's armor shattered to pieces. Daniel growled, as he got up from the ground. Spider Crusader tried to get up, but stumbled on to the ground. Spider Crusader said, "Leave me behind, I am too weak to continue fighting." Daniel said, "I can't leave you behind!" Spider Crusader said, "I will slow you down, the city needs an hero." Norman threw an grenade at Daniel and Spider Crusader. Daniel went in to his ghost form, and turned invisible. The grenade bounced through Daniel, and exploded in front of Spider Crusader. The explosion shattered the foundation of Oasis Falls High School, and the foundation collapsed on top of Spider Crusader, as he laid next to the shattered healing tube in an puddle of blood. Daniel walked over, and saw Spider Crusader's body, soaked in blood. Daniel growled in anger, as his body turned visible. Daniel flew in his ghost form toward Norman. Daniel grabbed Norman by his neck, and flew through the debris of Oasis Falls High School in to the sky. Daniel's eyes glowed green, as he ghost wailed Norman in to the ground. Norman smashed through the sky in to Zoomopolis. Norman laid on the ground, in an puddle of blood. Daniel landed in front of Norman's body, as his eyes returned to normal. Daniel analyzed Norman's body, and noticed there was an device on his wrist. The device exploded and the explosion pushed Daniel in to the car. The car and Daniel flew out of Zoomopolis, and landed in the forest. The explosion from Norman's body covered Zoomopolis, and destroyed the entire city. Zoomopolis was left in ruins, as the remains of the city laid on the ground. Daniel rubbed his hand, as he got up from the ground. Daniel went in to his ghost form, and flew toward the ruins of the city. Daniel landed on the ground, as he walked through the destruction. Various bodies laid on the ground in puddles of blood, while Daniel walked through the shattered glass and building rubble on the ground. Daniel went in to his ghost form, and flew out of Zoomopolis. Daniel flew in to the woods, and found an cabin. Daniel landed in front of the cabin. Daniel walked in to the cabin, and decided to make the cabin his new home. The cabin had an supply of food and water, since there was an huge lake in front of it. Daniel walked out of the cabin, and sat on the stairs. The squirrels ran toward Daniel, and hugged his legs. Daniel petted the squirrels, and smiled at them.

Josh Zimmer is an crazy individual with an extreme imagination. He loves to have fun by listening to music, writing stories, and playing video games of various genres such as platforming, multiplayer online games, role playing games, and sports games. His favorite technology brands are Nintendo and Microsoft. They are wonderful role models for the industry. He commands an army of cats to his will with hugs, love, and snacks. He makes the cats purr and meow with happiness.